PRAISE FOR
**TALES OF THE BLACK PHOENIX:
LOOPY IN LOVE**
BY ALLAN KEMP

"This is the greatest book ever written since the dawn of man!"
-Someone you've never heard of

"This book changed my life!"
-Someone even more obscure

"I wouldn't wipe my ass with this book!"
-Jealous ex-friend from high school who opted for a boring life working a dead-end job with a wife, two kids, and a house in the suburbs instead of reaching for the stars.

"HULK READ! Hulk touched by the depiction of the delicate balance between man's struggle for identity and the harsh realities of every day existence."
-Unauthorized blurb from the Incredible Hulk

"Is there no end to this nonsense?"
-A concerned friend

TALES OF THE BLACK PHOENIX:
LOOPY IN LOVE

ALLAN KEMP

Contact info

Email: theallankemp@mail.com

Twitter: @theallankemp

Website: http://www.theallankemp.com/home.html

Cover art by Sierra Ellison

Inside art by Mickey Dubrow

Copyright © 2016 by Mickey Dubrow

ISBN-13: 978-0997035216
ISBN-10: 0997035218

First Edition

WELCOME TO THE BLACK PHOENIX.

In a world ruled by the supernatural, there are still some places where everyone is welcome. One of those places is The Black Phoenix nightclub owned by wizard-werepanther Mutt Davidson in the heart of downtown Atlanta. Here wizards, witches, vampires, werewolves, ghosts, and humans are welcome to come in to listen to the DJ's music and enjoy the mood-altering substance of their choice. The only rule is that everyone is treated equally and no one is allowed to kill, eat, or enslave a fellow customer.

Mutt has met all kinds of people at the club and they all have a story to tell. These are the Tales of the Black Phoenix brought to you by your host, Mutt. So sit back, order a drink and try not to kill, eat, or enslave anybody.

CHAPTER ONE

I have no one to blame but myself for getting involved in K-9 Loopy's quest. He'd fallen in love and asked me to help him seduce the object of his affection.

"Why me?" I asked.

"You get more ass in a week than most wolves get in a month," K-9 said. "You get your dick wet so often I bet it's wet now."

He was wrong. At the moment, my dick was bone dry. It was true that I got a lot of ass, but that was because I was a popular DJ and I owned the Black Phoenix nightclub. That was casual sex, a string of one-nighters. I was a total loser when it came to long-term relationships that involved the word "love."

Still, I agreed to help K-9. Call it a cat thing. I was curious to see who had won his heart, because for as long as I had known this werewolf the only thing he truly loved was marijuana.

He was a connoisseur of cannabis. He could lecture for hours about the opposing benefits of Sativa and Indica plants. He was an expert on the planting and cultivation of primo Kush. He could create a bong out of just about anything. I could count on one hand the number of times when he didn't reek of pot.

What she wolf could have possibly competed with such slavish devotion to the magic herb? She must have been something truly magnificent to pull K-9's head out of his perpetual cloud of marijuana smoke.

"What's the girl's name?" I asked.

"Venus."

"Where did you find her?"

"Dawgie Daddy's. You used to work there. I thought maybe you knew her."

I remembered a Starr, a Moonchild, and a Sunshyne, but not a Venus. That wasn't surprising. Over two years had passed since I last performed at Dawgie's club, plenty of time for him to have a complete turnover of strippers.

"Guys to fall in love with the dancers all the time," I said. "But remember that you pay them to take off their clothes and have sex with you. What you think is true love could be nothing more than a business transaction to them."

K-9 yanked the bong we were sharing from my hands and gave me a dirty look. He'd built the bong from a carrot, a coffee pot, and duct tape.

"This is the real thing, you feel me?" he said. "I have fucked many bitches in my time, but with her it was different. We may have started out having a business transaction, but then we connected on a molecular level that was cosmic and revolutionary. Venus is my one and only."

"If you made a connection, then she must feel the same about you."

K-9 sucked on the carrot, the weed crackled, and the water in the pot burbled. He exhaled and I couldn't tell if the tears in his eyes were from the smoke or his yearning heart.

"I don't know shit about how to treat a bitch right," he said. "That's why I need your help."

"Have you tried asking her out on a date?"

I could tell by his blank stare that the thought had never entered his mind. Maybe I was qualified to help him after all.

"That's a good idea. I got to get some money first. I want to impress her."

"Actually, the first thing you should do is take a bath. I have found that women prefer a man who doesn't smell like a dead dog."

K-9 sniffed his underarm and more tears came to his eyes.

"Damn, Mutt. All this time, I thought that terrible smell was coming from you."

CHAPTER TWO

I spent two weeks with K-9 Loopy teaching him the art of romance. I suggested ways he could impress a girl that would make her feel special. Give her a gift for no reason. Bring her flowers. Compliment her shoes. Treat her with respect.

"Respect?" K-9 asked. "Don't spending money on the bitch show I respect her ass?"

"Spending money on her is nice, but that's not what I meant," I said. "Show that you respect her by treating her as your equal. Let her know that you think of her as something more than just the owner of the orifices for you jism."

"I can do that. I respect my momma. That proves I can respect a bitch."

"That's another thing. Try not to refer to Venus as a bitch."

"But technically, she is a bitch."

"No. A female dog is a bitch. A female wolf is a she wolf. So avoid calling her a bitch. In fact, avoid calling her things like ho, slut, and skank."

"What about chicken head, cunt, and deuce?"

"No, no, and no."

"What about cum dumpster?"

"Definitely, no!"

Finally, I felt like it was time for K-9 to go a practice date. The Black Phoenix was closed Mondays, so on Monday night I set a table in the middle of the empty club with linen and silverware. I couldn't convince any of my female friends to stand in for Venus, so I had Timothy play her part. Considering that most werewolves were extremely homophobic, I was pleased that K-9 didn't object. He treated Timothy as if he were Venus.

K-9 cleaned up well. He had ditched his usual fluorescent orange tennis shoes for a pair of polished black wingtips. He wore a burgundy vested sharkskin suit. He'd gotten a fade haircut and smelled of cologne instead of weed.

I played the waiter and led K-9 and Timothy to their table. K-9 sat down, but Timothy stood by his chair and waited.

"You don't like this table?" K-9 said. "We can sit someplace else. I'm not particular."

"He's waiting for you to pull out his chair," I said.

"Do women really like that shit?"

"The more you treat a girl like a queen," Timothy said. "The more she'll act like a whore when you get her home."

"How would you know?"

"Girls tell gay boys things they would never tell their boyfriends."

K-9 shrugged, got up, and pulled out Timothy's chair.

"Why thank you," Timothy said as he sat. "You're such a gentleman."

I brought them food and drinks. Well, I brought K-9 food, leftover spaghetti that I'd made for myself the night before. Vampires don't eat solid food so I brought Timothy a glass of red wine. K-9 dug into the spaghetti like he hadn't eaten in weeks, slurping the noodles loudly and splattering tomato sauce on his face.

"You might want to come up for air long enough to talk to your date," I said.

K-9 gulped down his glass of wine and belched.

"There's something I've been wondering about, Venus," he said. "How come you and the other Dawgie Daddy dancers won't do blowjobs? I mean, I enjoy fucking, but I like to get my dick sucked too."

I was about to smack the side of K-9's head, but Timothy handled the situation for me.

"I came out tonight to have some fun, not talk about work. How would you feel if I asked you how you get away with selling stink weed when there's plenty of good pot around?"

K-9 used his napkin to wipe tomato sauce off his chin.

"You're right. We're supposed to be getting to know each other. Tell me about yourself. Which pack do you run with? What's your favorite animal to hunt?"

Timothy leaned forward and rested his chin in his hands.

"That's much better. Everybody likes to talk about themselves. Ask her a few questions and she should take it from there."

"I can do that."

"And you seem to want to know her better."

"I want to know everything about her, what makes her smile, what makes her cry, what she likes for to eat when she's got the munchies. All that shit."

Timothy looked at me. "I think he's going to be fine," he said. He looked back at K-9. "If Venus won't suck your dick after this date, come see me."

CHAPTER THREE

It was a rainy night in Georgia. I felt like it was raining all over the world. Sorry, Tony Joe White. I couldn't resist. Dark clouds had hung over Atlanta all afternoon and when the sun went down the rain began. Buckets and buckets of rain fell on the city, flooding the sewers and the drainpipes.

Ed left before it started raining. He said he was going to spend a few days visiting friends. He didn't specify which friends. He was an earth spirit in the shape on an oversized tabby cat and had been around for eons so he knew just about everybody.

Not surprisingly, the rain kept most of my customers away. Normally, the Black Phoenix was packed on a Friday night, but there were just a few diehard drinkers hunkered down at the bar.

I poured drinks while Pinky sat on a barstool and read *The Great Speckled Bird*, the newspaper put out by Atlanta's human population. Timothy sat at a table and gossiped with a vampire rent boy. It wasn't that long ago that Timothy was selling his ass at the Ponce. Then he came to work for me.

It was only recently that Atlanta started using money again. After the invasion, the city set up a barter system since most banks had been destroyed along with the power gird. An ATM doesn't work without electricity.

Worldwide reconstruction had progressed to the point where the paranormal controlled central government felt it was time to re-establish a monetary economy. Arguments broke out about whose face should be on the new currency. Paranormal leaders fought over who was the most worthy. Someone even floated a proposal of using illustrations of famous literary paranormals like Dracula, the Wolf Man, and the Wicked Witch of the West. Finally, it was agreed to just use existing money since there was already plenty of it lying around.

The only drawback was that the paranormals wouldn't allow humans to use money, forcing them to remain on a barter system. It was a way for the paranormals to remind the humans who was in charge.

The Black Phoenix didn't follow this new policy. We accepted barter items or money from paranormals or humans. If a werewolf wanted to pay for his beer with a goat, we took the goat and gave him a chicken. If a human paid for his martini with a twenty-dollar bill, we gave him change.

So, where was I? Oh yeah, it was a rainy night in Georgia and I felt like it was raining all over the world. Business was so slow that I was considering closing up early, but then K-9 Loopy showed up with his date.

I was shocked to see him. He'd told me that he was taking her out to dinner, but he didn't say anything about coming here. On any other night, I could understand why he might want to take a girl clubbing after dinner, but not on a stormy night like this.

K-9 and his date were soaking wet. They left puddles behind them as they trudged into the club. K-9 didn't have a raincoat and his suit looked like it had drowned. His wingtips were covered in mud. His date had on a light jacket that was probably quite stylish at the start of the evening. Her pink dress clung to her body like a second skin. Steam rose off the top of her head.

"Mutt," K-9 said, "this here is Venus."

"Pleased to meet you, Venus," I said.

She was petite. I assumed that she stopped growing taller sometime in the sixth or seventh grade. As for the rest of her body, it definitely kept developing. She had generous curves and mammoth breasts. The woman oozed sex so I could see why K-9 fell for her. But then, she opened her mouth and I began to have doubts.

"So this is the motherfucker you dragged me here to see?" Venus said.

"Yeah," K-9 said, his face melting with embarrassment. "He's a good friend of mine. He owns this club."

Venus looked around the nearly empty room.

"I heard this was the most popular club in town. Could've fooled me."

"I'm afraid you caught us on a slow night," I said. "Let me make it up to you with a complimentary bottle of champagne."

"I don't need no handouts," K-9 said. "I got plenty of money."

He pulled a fat bankroll out of his pocket and peeled off a soggy hundred-dollar bill and laid it on the bar. Venus rolled her eyes and I wondered if he had flashed that bankroll one too many times during their date tonight.

"Timothy," I said.

Timothy pulled himself away from his friend and sauntered over to the bar. He looked Venus over and gave K-9 a thumbs up.

"Show this nice couple to our VIP table."

"We don't have a…" Timothy caught himself. "Right. The VIP table. Please follow me."

Timothy had almost blurted out that we didn't have a VIP table. The Black Phoenix was all about treating everyone equally whether they were human or paranormal. Reserving a table for special patrons to receive special treatment was against everything we stood for.

But Timothy understood that I wanted to help K-9 impress Venus by pretending that K-9 was a very important person. He led them to the last booth in the club.

The Black Phoenix was in the Flatiron Building, Atlanta's oldest skyscraper. It was called the flat iron building because it's triangular shape reminded people of the household item used to iron clothes. The last booth in the club was at the narrow tip of the triangle and faced the rest of the club. Venus must have felt like a queen on her throne, looking out on her kingdom.

Timothy brought K-9 and Venus towels so that they could dry off and then he brought the champagne, popped it open, poured two glasses, and then left the bottle in a chilled bucket. So, they really did get VIP treatment.

After delivering the champagne, Timothy came to the bar and sat down next to Pinky.

"I don't see what K-9 sees in her," he said.

"Big tits?" Pinky said.

"Is that really all a straight boy needs? That girl is such a demanding bitch. She gave me a hard time about every little thing and she did everything she could to humiliate K-9. I've known a lot of prissy queens in my time, but this girl makes Queen Mayella look like Mother Teresa."

"I've seen Venus around," Pinky said. "She's a member of the Sister Alpha pack."

"The lesbian wolf pack?"

"Not all of them are lesbians. They're a pack of alpha female wolves. They don't take no shit from male wolves. K-9 doesn't seem like the type to go for that kind of she wolf."

"We don't always choose who we love," I said.

"I agree," Pinky said, "but something ain't right about this."

An hour passed during which I resisted the urge to spy on K-9 and Venus. K-9 came to the bar with his head down and his hands in his pockets.

"We need another bottle of champagne," he said.

"Sure," I said. "Timothy, would you mind getting that?"

"On it," Timothy said. He put his hand on K-9's shoulder. "Remember what I told you last week. If she won't give you a blowjob, I will."

K-9 stared at his shoes. Timothy giggled as he went to get the champagne and fresh glasses.

"Uh, Mutt, would you mind coming by the table?" K-9 said. "Venus feels bad that she was so rude earlier and wants to thank you personally for treating us so well."

I looked over at Pinky.

"Think you can hold down the fort while I'm gone?" I asked.

Pinky inspected the three barflies nursing their drinks.

"I think I can manage."

I came around the bar and started for K-9's table when I noticed that he hadn't moved.

"Are you coming?" I asked.

"I have to hit the can first. I'll catch up with you."

I figured he needed a break from Venus, so I went to his table without him. I passed the stage and threaded my way between empty tables. Venus greeted with a big friendly smile that made me feel like a fly about to land in a spider's web. I scooted into the booth and she shuffled her ample butt over next to me. Her dress was still damp and plastered to her well-rounded body. She put her warm hand on mine and looked up at me with her big brown eyes.

"K-9 told me that you own this entire building," she said.

"I own the whole block and the park across the street."

"Damn, you must be rich!"

"I do okay. Keep in mind that the city gave me the deeds to all this property when no one else wanted anything to do with downtown. They would've given me all of downtown Atlanta if I had wanted it."

"The city gave all this to you? For free?"

"Yeah. I was determined to rebuild this area. For a year, the Black Phoenix was the only business here."

Venus' eyes fluttered and she put her hand over her large breasts. I thought she was about to have a heart attack.

"Downtown is the fastest growing area in the city. Just on this block, you've got a Mexican restaurant, a produce market, and a hardware store. How much rent are you charging them?"

"I'm not charging them anything. They're all struggling to get their businesses off the ground. The more successful they are, the more it benefits me, and the faster this area grows."

Venus downed the last of the champagne in her glass and fanned herself.

"Oh no! That's got to change. You got to get the money up front. They'll tell you that they don't have the money to pay you, but they do."

I slipped my hand away from Venus' and squeezed her knee.

"Don't worry about it, Venus. It's my business."

"This building has eleven floors. Please tell you're renting out the floors above the club."

"The first two floors are for the club and I live on the top floor. Other than when friends come to visit, the rest of the floors are empty because I prefer them to be empty."

"You may be a great DJ but you don't shit about business. Put me in charge and I'll make you a very rich man in no time."

I squeezed her knee tighter.

"I appreciate the advice, but like I said. It's my business."

I thought she'd either take the hint and back off or she'd try to smack me, so I braced myself for either reaction. Instead, she spread her legs and pulled my hand down to her crotch.

"You're so forceful," she purred. "Okay, I won't get in your business no more, but maybe we can get up into something else."

She pushed my hand down deeper. Either her panties were still damp from the rain or the moisture was coming from another source. My dick got hard. I didn't want it to get hard, but I could smell her werewolf pussy, one of the most powerful scents in the supernatural world. My mind was yelling run away this she wolf wants to eat you alive, but my body was saying come on one little fuck wont' hurt.

"What about K-9?" I asked weakly.

"I'm sure you can take care of him if he becomes a problem."

To my great relief, Timothy arrived with the champagne. I retrieved my hand from between Venus' legs. Timothy pursed his lips at me with disapproval and I glared back at him.

"Have you seen K-9?" I asked. "He said he was going to the bathroom. Even if he was taking a dump, he should be done by now."

Timothy opened the champagne with a loud pop. As he filled Venus' glass, he said, "Mutt, you're needed at the bar."

I bolted out of the booth.

"Bar owner's work is never done. I'll be right back, Venus."

I walked with Timothy.

"I don't see what the hell K-9 sees in her," I said.

I was bent over to hide my erection, but Timothy noticed it anyway.

"It looked like you were about to see a lot more of her."

"She found out I owned this block and thought she could fuck her way into part ownership."

"Well now I almost like her."

"Thanks for getting me away from that crazy bitch."

"You're welcome, but we really do have a situation."

"Really? What's up?"

"K-9 has left the building. Pinky saw him haul ass out the back door."

"Can't say I blame him. Five more minutes with Venus and I would have been right behind him."

"It wasn't Venus that made him run. It was the two huge werewolves who showed up looking for him. He must have seen them coming because he left right before they entered the club."

I didn't see them until we passed the stage. They were in human form, but we paranormals don't need to see fur and a tail to identify a werewolf. They were huge, scary looking motherfuckers. They saw me coming and gave me their coldest you're-a-dead-man stare.

"What did you tell them?" I asked.

"I told them K-9 wasn't here," Timothy said.

"Then why are they still here?"

"They want to talk to you. For some reason, they think you and K-9 are partners."

My feet refused to keep walking. The two werewolves didn't mind. They came to me.

CHAPTER FOUR

They were identical twins, which meant they were equally ugly. One of them smacked his right fist into his left palm repeatedly; a threatening gesture that went out of style around the same time men stopped wearing garters to hold up their socks. The one not smacking his fist began the conversation.

"Where's K-9 Loopy?"

"I have no idea. He left without saying goodbye."

"You're his business partner, so we'll deal with you."

"I'm his friend, but I'm not his partner."

"But he said you were."

"He lied. Could you at least explain what this is all about?"

He nodded at his twin.

"Show him, Remi."

Remi took a joint out of his shirt pocket and handed it to me.

"Smoke it," he said.

Whoever rolled this joint did a poor job. It was lumpy with stems poking through the paper. I sniffed it and frowned. It didn't have that sweet tangy marijuana scent. It smelled like mildew. Remi lit a match and held it toward me. I grimaced before putting the nasty thing in my mouth. The match set fire to the other end and I inhaled. Immediately, I coughed out the smoke.

"That is some nasty shit," I said.

"Damn right," Remi said.

"This is stink weed!" I said, holding the joint at arm's length.

"This is what K-9 sold us. Said it was the best sensimilla he'd come across in years. He gave us a sample that knocked us on our ass, and then he took our money and left us a kilo of this crap."

"No wonder you want to kick his ass. I want to kick his ass just for putting me in a position where I had to taste this disgusting shit."

Remi grabbed my shirt and pulled me up until my feet dangled in the air. He held me close to his face and I got the full force of his rancid breath.

"You're K-9's partner. Give us back our money or we break you in half."

"Remi," I said calmly. "Can I call you Remi? I don't allow fighting in the bar so I suggest we continue this conversation outside."

"I'll do whatever the fuck I want to do."

"If we don't go outside, then a vampire is going to kill your brother and a werewolf is going to kill you."

Remi looked over at his brother. He stood perfectly still, except for his eyes nervously darting back and forth. Timothy's arms and legs were wrapped around the large man and his vampire teeth were extended, the sharp points pressed against the twin's neck. Pinky was beside Remi with a handgun pointed at his head.

"This gun is loaded with silver bullets," Pinky said. "If you don't believe me, I'll be more than happy to prove it to you."

Remi slowly lowered me to the ground.

"If you hadn't come in here acting like lowlife gangsters, I would have offered you a drink and we could have discussed some kind of resolution to your problem," I said as I smooth my shirt. "Instead, you're going to get your asses kicked for no good reason. Please follow me."

I marched outside with the twins close behind me. Pinky, Timothy, and the three barflies followed us and lined up on the sidewalk to watch the fight. I didn't see Venus. She was in a remote corner of the club so she probably wasn't aware of what was going on.

Peachtree Street was empty. The other businesses on the block were closed. The rain had tapered down to a light drizzle making the air feel sticky. We faced off like gunslingers with the twins at one end of the street and lonesome me on the other. They transformed, ripping their clothes off in the process. As men, they were big and ugly. As werewolves, they were bigger and uglier. Their fur was shit brown and dull. Their snouts looked like they had run face first into a brick wall. They snarled, gnashed their teeth, and flexed their paws. I did nothing.

I could have transformed and used my combined wizard and werepanther powers to turn them into a grease spot on the road, but that didn't seem fair. K-9 had cheated them. They had a legitimate beef, just not with me. I wanted to make them go away without hurting them. They didn't know it, but I had already cast the spell that would do just that.

As we were taking our positions on the street, I cast an invisible protection bubble. Only I didn't put the bubble around me. I put it around the werewolf twins. If they hadn't been concentrating on me, they might have noticed that the bubble was keeping the drizzle out. It was like they were in a snow globe with the snow outside the globe.

When they finally got tired of waiting for me to transform, they rushed toward me intending no doubt to rip me to shreds. They hit the invisible barrier and bounced back, which caused the bubble to bounce, which caused them to bump into each other, which caused the bubble to bounce even more. The crowd on the sidewalk laughed as the bubble went up and down as if it were a rubber ball, tossing the twins around inside. They tried bursting the bubble with their claws, but my spell was too strong.

I cast a spell to hold the bubble steady. The werewolves got to their feet and pressed their snouts against the invisible barrier.

"When I get out of this, I'm going to rip your head off and shove it up your ass," snarled Remi.

"I'm going to tear out your liver and make you watch me eat it," said his brother.

"Look guys," I said. "I'm really sorry that K-9 ripped you off, but I was telling you the truth. I have nothing to do with this deal."

"I'm going to fuck your skull!"

"I'm going to burn down your fucking bar."

I had tolerated the nasty things they said they were going to do to me, but when they threatened the Black Phoenix, I lost my temper. I put my hand on the bubble and cast a spell to siphon the air out. It escaped out of the top of the globe and blew a path through the drizzle.

The werewolves gasped and held their throats. They pounded on the barrier in desperation. They fell to their knees. Their mouths tried to suck in what little air was left.

"Where's your big talk now?" I sneered. "Come on. Tell me what kind of bad ass shit you're going to do to me."

I felt Pinky's strong hand squeeze my shoulder.

"You're killing them, Mutt," he said. "Is that really what you want to do?"

The werewolves were on the ground, weakly pawing the barrier. I quickly cast a counter spell that filled the bubble with air. They breathed it in deeply into their ravaged lungs.

"Fuck me," I said. "I almost ended those poor assholes."

Pinky patted my back.

"It's okay. They pushed your buttons."

"That's no excuse. I fucked up."

"You did, but we still love you."

I hugged Pinky. Timothy ran over and joined us. I don't think he cared that I almost killed the twins; he just liked group hugs.

"So what are you going to do with them?" Timothy asked.

"I'm going to do this."

I cast a spell for a breeze to pick up the bubble and carry it away. The werewolves cowered inside. Remi barked and the puke splattered on the side and dribbled to the floor. His brother slipped on the mess.

The three barflies on the sidewalk applauded.

"What's going to happen to them?" Pinky asked.

"They'll float for a few miles and then the bubble will land softly and pop like a big soap bubble."

"Where is it going to land?"

"Fuck if I know. That's their problem."

We returned to the bar. I poured everybody a drink and we toasted the bubble and wished it a safe journey.

"All right," I said. "That was enough excitement for one night. I'm closing up."

The three barflies moaned, but left without argument. Pinky, Timothy, and I closed down the bar. Pinky headed out, but Timothy lagged behind.

"Aren't you forgetting something?" Timothy said.

"Oh shit," I said, slapping my forehead. "I forgot about Venus."

"Want me to help you throw her out?"

"We can't do that. She's just like those werewolves. K-9 screwed her. I'll offer her a ride home."

"Are you sure that's all you'll offer her?"

Timothy thrust his hips in a suggestive way.

"Get the fuck out of here," I said, giving him a friendly push.

He was still laughing as he walked out the door.

CHAPTER FIVE

When I got to Venus' table, I found an empty champagne bottle swimming in a bucket of melted ice, but no sign of Venus. Her jacket was on the seat so I figured she must be in the bathroom after drinking all that liquid, but then music started blasting out of the sound system.

I made my way to the stage. The stage lights came on and Venus walked out. The music was slinky with a hard thumping beat. My first reaction was anger because she'd messed with my sound and lighting system without asking. She probably made a mess of my carefully organized mixtapes. My second and calmer reaction was that if Venus wanted to put on a show, then put on a show. There were worse things in life than watching a woman with a great body show off what nature had given her. I took a front row seat.

Venus swung her hips to the beat while her fingers tickled the air. Her hands snaked up and down her body, pausing to squeeze her breasts before traveling over her belly and continuing south to rub her crotch. She turned her back to me and gyrated her generous ass.

She reached behind her and unzipped her pink dress. She slowly peeled it off her shoulders, rolled it over her breasts, and pushed it past her hips before letting the dress fall to the floor where it landed in a soft heap. She stepped out of it and continued her dance.

I was impressed that her bra and panties matched. More than a decade had passed since the invasion, but many industries had not recovered, including the clothing industry. The only new clothes were handmade and nobody I knew of was hand stitching bras and panties. Venus must have saved these undergarments for special occasions only.

They were blood red. The bra was lacy with a tiny fabric rose stitched between the cups. It looked too fragile to contain her ginormous tits. The thong panties barely covered her vagina and the back strap disappeared between her massive butt cheeks.

Venus danced across the stage and then came down the stairs to the main floor. She sashayed over to me and gave me a lap dance. She mashed her breasts in my face and then turned and dragged her round ass across my crotch. I worried that K-9 was going to show up at any moment, see Venus rubbing her parts on me, and be heartbroken. But my dick said fuck it this bitch was hot, and got harder than a diamond.

She stopped dancing and stood over me with her legs spread apart. She reached back causing her breasts to strain against the flimsy fabric holding them in place and in one deft motion unhooked her bra. She wrapped her arms over her tits as one bra strap slipped off her shoulder followed by the other strap. A wicked smile spread across her lips as she removed the bra and draped it over my shoulder. She stood before me in nothing but her red thong panties and a pair of glittery red fuck me pumps. She tweaked her dark brown nipples until they were erect.

She kneeled down between my legs and quickly loosened my belt, unzipped my jeans, and yanked them and my boxer shorts down to my ankles. I felt a light breeze as my dick stood at attention.

"Why are you doing this?" I asked.

She put her finger on my lips and then licked hers. Like the best magic trick ever, she made my dick disappear inside her mouth. Instead of applause, I groaned with pleasure. She sucked me long enough to get my dick slick with her spit. She pushed my legs further apart and got on her knees. She lifted her breasts, placed my dick between them, and then squished them together.

I love pussy and the smell of her werewolf pussy was driving me crazy, but I also love a good tit fuck. I resisted the urge to transform and take her from behind. Her breasts were soft and warm as my dick glided in and out. Every time my dick popped out at the top of her cleavage, she licked the head.

A few more strokes and I was ready to explode. Venus sensed that I was at the point of no return and pressed the sides of her breasts to hold my dick more snuggly. I thrust my hips faster, my ass lifting off the chair as I gripped the sides to keep from falling off. Right before I came, I looked down at her face. She was smiling at me. It wasn't a loving or sexy smile. It was a smirk that said she had conquered me.

I tried to hold back, but it was too late. My dick erupted and I blasted her tits with cum. The white goo bubbled out of the top of her cleavage and stuck to her chin.

I relaxed and waited for my ears to stop ringing. Venus leaned back and inspected the globs of cum on her breasts. She scooped some with her finger and stuck it in her mouth.

"Will you make me your business partner now?" she said.

I pulled up my pants and shuffled away from her.

"There's a bathroom over there," I said, pointing. "Clean up and get dressed. It doesn't look like your boyfriend is coming back so I'll take you home."

Venus narrowed her eyes and scrambled to her feet. With an angry howl, her breasts flattened into animal sinew and muscle as she transformed. Her ears grew into rounded mounds on the top of her head as fur covered her body. Claws sprang from her hands and feet. She towered over me, her yellow eyes filled with hate. And then, she swatted me with her powerful arm. My head hit the wood floor. Pain blossomed inside my skull and traveled to the rest of my body. My shoulder ached from where her claws raked me. I rolled onto my back and tried to focus. She stood over me and snarled.

I hurt and I wanted to hurt her back. I clenched my fists and imagined blasting the bitch into a bloody mist.

I took a deep breath to calm myself. Though Venus' claws were inches from my throat, I didn't believe she wanted to kill me. Just because she lost her temper was no reason for me to lose mine. Besides, I'd faced too many werewolves to be intimidated. I took a moment to admire her beautiful coat of silver and black.

"So if you can't seduce me into doing business with you, you'll rip my head off instead?" I asked.

Venus snapped her jaws shut. She stepped away from me and transformed back to human. There was still anger in her eyes, but now it was mixed with shame. She reached between her butt cheeks and pulled out a strip of red fabric, all that was left of her thong panties. Pouting, she picked her matching red bra and pink dress off the dirty floor. Storming across the club, she opened the bathroom door and hesitated.

"K-9 ain't my boyfriend!" she shouted before slamming the door shut.

CHAPTER SIX

I checked my arm where Venus had scratched me. Her claws had ripped my shirt and left bloody trails in my flesh. They stung when I touched them. The ragged grooves weren't too deep. She must have been holding back.

I went to the bar and took out the first aid kit I kept on hand in case somebody managed to get himself hurt. I had a vial filled with a magic potion I'd cooked up that rapidly heals wounds. I took off my shirt and rubbed the sticky black goo over the cut. I felt a tingling sensation as the wound closed up. I went to my office for a new shirt and left the torn one on my desk as a reminder to mend it later.

I waited outside the bathroom for over an hour before Venus emerged. I fought the urge to stare at her crotch since I knew she wasn't wearing panties. She must have washed down there because I didn't smell the intoxicating scent of werewolf pussy.

I handed her coat to her. She slung it over her arm.

"If we're going to go, then let's go," she said.

"My truck is parked in the alley."

"Oh no. I'm not walking in these shoes in some nasty ass alley."

Her glittery high heels already had mud on them, but I knew better than to argue with a woman about her shoes.

"Fine," I said. "You wait out front and I'll drive around."

I took the back door to the alley. My truck was parked about fifteen yards away. The rain clouds had blown away and I could see the moon, a sliver of pale blue. I trudged along and wondered what the hell did K-9 see in Venus. He was a laid back stoner and she was a shark willing to do anything to make a deal.

I didn't find Venus' behavior repulsive. It was her hard sell approach that I found annoying. The supernatural were told by their leaders that the invasion would turn the world into a supernatural paradise. It did for the leaders but not so much for soldiers like Venus and K-9 Loopy. They could get a human slave to cook their meals, but they still had to buy the food. That meant the supernatural who weren't leaders had to find jobs, which were scarce because human slave labor did most of the work that needed to be done for free.

I was so deep in thought about how the invasion had created an economic meltdown that I didn't notice that someone was behind me until it was too late. I heard a small splash of water and didn't think anything about it. But then, I smelled the pungent zing of ozone and heard an electric crackle, which told me I was about to be hit by a stinger spell.

I dived and the spell missed me by inches. I landed in a puddle. My clothes were wet and sticky, but I was in one piece. I cast a protective shield around me. The next stinger spell came seconds after the first one and almost destroyed the shield.

My assailant hung back in the shadows on the other side of the alley. If she knew anything about me, then she would have known that I had the night vision of a panther. I could see that she a witch with short blonde hair. She was a cute blue jean femme whom I'd never seen before, which begged the question: why was she trying to burn my ass?

I figured the best way to find out was to ask.

"Hey Blondie," I said. "Why are you trying to burn my ass?"

Panic spread across her face as she touched her hair. She cast a fireball spell at me that hit the shield and burst into a wall of fire. I cast a counter spell that put the fire out, but created a blinding cloud of black smoke. By the time it floated away, the witch had escaped.

Confused and aching, I got in the truck and drove around the block to the front of the building. Venus was pacing impatiently. When she saw me, she put her fists on her hips and tapped her foot. I parked, got out, and opened the passenger door for her.

"What the fuck took you so damn long?" she said. "And why do you stink like you been sleeping in a sewer?"

"I ran into some trouble."

She climbed into the truck.

"I don't want to hear about it. I want to get home before this night can get any worse."

Little did we know that the night would get worse and that taking Venus home wouldn't make it any better.

CHAPTER SEVEN

Venus talked business during the entire drive to her home. The girl was obsessed with running a business. She explained that it was her destiny because nobody was more qualified to create a financial empire than her. All she needed was someone to give her the reins of their business and then sit back and watch the profit margins rise. Her slamming me to the floor had given me a headache and her non-stop sales pitch made it worse. There was a sharp pain in my forehead right above my left eyebrow.

I'll admit that I didn't have a good head for business. The Black Phoenix turned a profit because it was the only nightclub in the downtown area. A monkey could run the place as well as I did. Okay, that was insulting to monkeys. But I wasn't trying to make a profit. I just wanted to provide a place where humans and paranormals could hang out together without fear of being attacked, eaten, or burned at the stake.

Venus lived in the Bluff Village. To get to her house, we had to drive by the remains of the Pound. The Pound was a walled off city block and was once home to the now defunct werewolf pack, the Young Wolfz. I hated driving by the burned out buildings and crumbling walls because I was partly responsible for their destruction. Seeing the devastated Pound brought back painful memories and left a sour taste in my mouth.

We drove past and a mile later Venus directed me to take a right followed by a left onto a gravel road lined with dilapidated houses.

"See that yellow house?" Venus said. "That's my place."

Venus pointed at a two-story house with peeling vinyl siding. There were no lights on inside. The front yard had a beautiful oak tree and enough weeds to hide an army. There were oily black splotches on the driveway to show that cars did reside there occasionally. I parked on the street and waited for Venus to get her big butt out of my truck.

"Aren't you going to walk me to the front door?" she asked.

"K-9 was your date tonight. Let him do it."

"If his weak ass was here, I would. Now walk me to my damn door."

I got out and escorted Venus to her house. I had no intention of giving her a good night kiss. She put her hand on the doorknob and sighed. She looked tired and sad. I felt sorry for her. She might have been a pain in the ass, but she didn't deserve to get dumped by her date.

"Well, this night wasn't a complete disaster," she said.

"Really? How so?"

"You got to bust a nut and didn't make fun of my name."

"Why would I make fun of your name? Because Venus is the goddess of love?"

"No. Venus Flytrap. I hate when people call me that."

"Well, good night. Maybe I'll see you around."

"Once I go inside, I doubt I'll ever see you again."

"You're probably right."

She opened the door and a large hand reached out and yanked her inside. I was too surprised to move and then I couldn't move because there was a double barrel shotgun pointed at my chest.

Remi held the shotgun and judging by the shit-eating grin on his face aiming his weapon at me made him very happy.

"Both barrels are loaded with silver pellet buckshot. You might have magic powers, but I'm guessing you can't stop this shit from tearing a big hole in your chest."

"You guessed right," I said.

"What you standing outside in the cold for? Come in and join the party."

I went inside the house. The place smelled like someone had left a package of raw bacon and a sweaty jockstrap in a gym locker for five years. With the shotgun pressed to my back, Remi led me to the living room. There was a couch and two leather recliners. Duct tape covered multiple rips in the fabric. Venus sat on the couch and crossed her arms and legs. Remi's twin brother entered the room carrying a straight back chair and silver chains. He put the chair in the middle of the room.

"Sit down," Remi ordered, nudging me with the shotgun.

I stared at Venus, but she avoided my gaze. I sat in the chair. Remi's twin tied my hands behind my back with the silver chains.

"I never did get your name," I said to him as he chained my ankles to the legs of the chair.

"That's Rom," Venus said.

"Rom and Remi. Is that short for Romulus and Remus?"

"That's right."

I smiled at Remi. He didn't smile back.

"Either your parents were big fans of Greek mythology or they believed the legend that Romulus and Remus were the original werewolves."

"Shut the fuck up," Rom said as he smacked the back of my head.

Rom's love tap didn't help my throbbing headache any. I could feel it burrowing from the back of my head to my nose.

"You must know the story of Romulus and Remus?" I said. "Romulus kills Remus."

Remi crossed the room and pressed the shotgun barrels against my forehead. I strained to pull my hands free, but the silver chains cut into my skin. A trickle of blood touched the silver sending a burning sensation from my wrists to my toes. My mouth went dry.

"You got something else to say?" Remi said. I didn't answer and he laughed. "I didn't think so."

He eased the shotgun away from my head and sat in a recliner. Rom sat in the other recliner. Venus sprung off the couch and stomped her heel on the floor.

"Somebody tell me what the fuck is going on?" she said.

"You didn't plan this?" I asked.

"I didn't plan shit. These are my brothers."

Venus, Romulus, and Remus. Damn, their parents really were into Greek mythology.

"This motherfucker ripped us off," Rom said. "Sold us a kilo of stink weed."

"I didn't sell you shit," I said. "How many times do I have to tell you that I'm not K-9 Loopy's partner."

"Whoa, whoa, whoa," Venus said, holding up her hands. "What does K-9 got to do with Mutt and a kilo of stink weed?"

"Apparently, K-9 sold your brothers a kilo of inferior product," I said. "It would seem that he also told them I was his business partner. They came by the Black Phoenix with the intention of forcing me to give them their money back. I cast a spell that made them go away."

"When did this happen?"

"Tonight."

"Where was I when you were casting spells on my brothers?"

"Drinking champagne at the VIP table. By the way, it's not really a VIP table. We called it that to make you feel special."

"Where the fuck was K-9?"

"From what I understand, he saw your brothers coming and made a run for it."

Venus held her forehead as if she were checking to see if she had a fever.

"There's something I don't understand," I said.

"There are many things I don't understand, but I'm going to find out," Venus said.

"Why didn't you know that K-9 sold weed to your brothers? You all live in the same house. For that matter, why didn't Rom and Remi confront K-9 when he came to pick you up for your date?"

"Venus Flytrap!" Remi said. "You're dating K-9?"

"I told you not to call me that," Venus said. "It was just one date and since when has it been any business of yours who the hell I go out with? As for K-9, he picked me up tonight at Dawgie Daddy's."

"Why didn't you have him pick you up here?" Rom asked. "You ashamed of us?"

"Yes, I am ashamed of you losers, but that's not why. I worked the afternoon shift. No reason to go home before the date. Now, tell me. How much did you spend for that kilo?"

Rom and Remi frowned at each other. Venus stomped her heel on the floor again.

"How much!" she shouted.

"Twelve thousand," Rom said.

"What the fuck were you thinking? The prices ain't like they were before the invasion. The most you can get for an ounce these days is $250.00 and that's for top of the line chronic. Even if you broke the kilo down to grams and quarter grams, the most you're going to make is around nine thousand. You overpaid that son of a bitch. That's why I keep telling you dumbasses to let me be your business manager."

"We can handle our business just fine," Remi said. "We don't need our little sister telling us what to do."

"Actually, you would be better off if you put her in charge," I said. "She obviously knows more about dealing weed than you guys."

Remi leaped out of his recliner and stomped across the room. He held the shotgun over his head as if he was going to slam the butt into my head. I flinched and Remi chuckled.

"You need to stop running your mouth," he said. "This is your last warning. Nod if you understand that I'm not playing?"

I nodded. Remi plopped back into his recliner. The poor idiot had no clue that I was playing the helpless victim for his benefit. I had already cast a spell on the silver chains that turned them into silver-colored string. I could slip them off easily. I also cast a spell to jam his shotgun. If he pulled the trigger, nothing would happen.

Rom and Remi were too stupid to be pot dealers and too arrogant to let Venus help them. It seemed pointless to hurt them when life had already kicked the shit out of them. I was waiting for an opportunity to escape without anybody getting hurt.

"So what's your master plan here?" Venus said. "How long you going to hold him?"

"It's not like we were expecting him to deliver his ass to our front door," Remi said.

"So you don't have a plan?"

"We have a plan," Rom said defensively. "A really good plan. Don't we, Remi?"

Remi nodded until he realized Venus was waiting for him to actually come up with a plan.

"Yeah," Remi said. "Here's what we're going to do. Venus, call K-9. Tell him we got his partner and if he wants to see him alive, then be here in thirty minutes with our money."

"What if K-9 doesn't show up with the money?" Venus said.

"Then we kill this motherfucker!"

"I don't know how I feel about that. Mutt is full of shit, but I don't know how I feel about killing him. Besides, I think he's telling the truth about not being K-9's partner."

"It doesn't matter what you think. You're our little sister so you got to do what we tell you to do."

"Bullshit! Hey, where did you get the money to buy that kilo? You guys are always borrowing money from me and never paying it back. Where did you get twelve thousand dollars?"

Rom and Remi hung their heads. Venus tapped her foot.

"We got it from your room," Remi said. "We know you hide your tips under your mattress."

Venus stumbled back and landed hard on the couch. She looked like she'd suddenly come down with a terrible disease.

"You took MY money? So tonight when K-9 was flashing that fat bankroll that was MY money. That means I paid him to take me out on the worse date of my life."

"Well, when you put it that way, it does sound kind of bad," Remi said.

"Somebody give me their phone so I can call K-9 to bring me my money."

"Don't you mean our money?"

"Just because you stole it from me doesn't make it your money. Now give me your goddamn phone."

Rom and Remi patted their pockets in search of a cell phone. Rom found his first and handed it to Venus.

"Remember to tell K-9 that if he ain't here in thirty minutes then we kill Mutt," Rom said.

Venus' fingers hovered over the keypad. She looked at me with the saddest expression. She had to decide between my life and her money. I wanted to tell her that she didn't need to make that decision because I wasn't in any danger. But then, the big oak tree in the front yard exploded. Maybe my life was in danger. Maybe all of our lives were in danger.

CHAPTER EIGHT

Out the living room window, I could see that the oak tree was in flames. Rom ran out of the room and came back holding a handgun in each hand. He and Remi rushed outside. The front door slammed and then I heard Remi shout, "Rom, the shotgun jammed. Give me one of your guns." "Get your own damn gun," Rom shouted back.

There was rapid gunfire followed by more explosions. I could tell from the crackling sound that preceded the explosions that someone was lobbing stinger spells at the twins. I hoped that one of them didn't hit my truck. With a sharp tug, the silver-colored strings snapped and I shook them off my wrists. I pulled the strings off my ankles and stood next to the window. Venus stared at me in disbelief.

"How'd you do that?" she asked. "You were tied up with silver. How come it didn't burn you?"

"I'm magic, remember?" I said. "Any idea who's attacking your house?"

Venus stood at the other side of the window.

"Stupid bitch. I loved that old oak tree."

I was going to ask Venus which stupid bitch she was talking about, though I had a feeling I had met her earlier this evening, when a bullet crashed through a window pane between us. Shards of glass littered the floor as we both hugged the wall.

"That wasn't a stinger spell," I said as I peeked out the window. "Somebody on the other side of the street is shooting at the house."

Venus peered out for a moment before retreating back to the wall.

"That's my lazy ass neighbors acting human," Venus said.

Normally when a werewolf felt the need to get involved in an altercation, he would transform and tackle the threat with claws and fangs. But then some werewolves decided it was easier to use an automatic weapon instead. These werewolves were considered lazy and an embarrassment to the werewolf community because humans relied on guns. The ultimate insult to any paranormal is to claim that they're acting human.

"Your brothers used a gun to take me hostage," I said.

"They're lazy, human acting motherfuckers too."

The mayhem in the front yard provided the perfect distraction for me to slip out. I headed toward the kitchen. Venus followed me.

"Where the hell are you going?" she asked.

"Home," I said. "I'll come back for the truck after you and your brothers resolve your beef with K-9."

The kitchen sink was full of dirty dishes. The floor hadn't seen a broom or a mop since before the invasion. A garbage can overflowing with empty cans and bottles sat by a door.

"Where does that lead to?" I asked. Venus crossed her arms and pouted. "Come on, Venus, you know I don't have anything to do with this. If I see K-9, I'll tell him to return your money."

Venus threw her hands in the air. "Okay, okay. The kitchen door leads out to the back yard.

There's an alley on the other side of the fence. I'm sure you'll figure out how to get hom from there."

The kitchen door busted open, knocking over the garbage can. Cans clattered and bottles shattered. K-9 looked at the mess he'd created on the kitchen floor and then looked at us. His burgundy vested sharkskin suit was caked with mud.

"I sneaked in to rescue you," he said.

"Good job," I said. "No way anyone would know you were here."

"Where's my damn money!" shouted Venus.

K-9 cocked his head to the side like a confused dog.

"We need to escape," he said. "Crazy motherfuckers live here."

"I couldn't agree more," I said.

"I don't need to escape," Venus said. "I just need my money. Now hand it over."

I grabbed her arm.

"He has no idea what you're talking about and the twins will be back before you can explain it to him."

"And your point is?"

"They might try to kill him once they get what they want. And if they do, then I might have to kill them first."

"You realize I'm standing right here," K-9 said. "And I still have no idea what the fuck you're talking about."

"Fine!" Venus said. "If it means getting my money back, then he can *rescue* me."

K-9 led the way to the back yard. He had removed two boards from the fence. He squeezed through first. Venus grunted as she squeezed her voluptuous body through the tight opening. Her dress caught on a nail and it ripped a slit down the side of her dress. Coming through the fence after her, I was reminded that she wasn't wearing panties.

"Damn," she said. "Now my coochie's hanging out for all the world to see."

As we ran to the end of the alley, I kept looking over my shoulder. The explosions and gunfire had died out. Soon Rom and Remi would find out that Venus and I were missing. K-9's car was parked two blocks away behind one of the last remaining churches for humans.

The car was a dirt-caked Land Rover. We piled in and K-9 turned the ignition. The car whined and refused to start. I kept watch as he coaxed the engine. Because the invasion halted production, all cars in the world were at least fifteen years old and there weren't many mechanics in business so having a car break down was nothing new. We just didn't need this one to die on us right now.

K-9 tried again and the engine roared to life.

"How did you know where to find us?" I asked as K-9 sped down the road.

"I came back to the Black Phoenix just as you and Venus were leaving," K-9 said. "I was upset that you moved in on my date, but then I did bug out on her."

"Damn right you did," Venus said.

"I was jealous so I followed you two. When you pulled up at Rom and Remi's, I figured you was going to buy some pot from them. I hid and watched.

When Rom and Remi forced ya'll inside, I decided to put my jealousy aside and rescue both of you."

"How did you manage to blow up the tree in the front yard and then get to the back yard without Rom and Remi seeing you?" I asked.

"I didn't have nothing to do with that. In fact, I was in the back yard trying to decide how to sneak in when that shit just happened."

I looked at Venus.

"Do you get the feeling there are things going on that we don't know about?"

She nodded.

"All the damn time."

CHAPTER NINE

K-9 meandered through Bluff Village, turning onto sides streets seemingly at random, and eventually ended up at the Pound. I was shocked when he drove through its rusted open gates and parked the car in the main square. The buildings along the edge of the square were burned out husks. They still carried a faint smell of charred wood. The place had been abandoned to bad memories.

"Here we are," K-9 said. "Home sweet home."

"Are you fucking out of your mind?" Venus said. "Nobody but ghosts live here."

"Give it a chance. The place grows on you."

Venus glared at me and I shrugged. I was a tourist here too. K-9 walked between the burnt buildings until we came upon a cinder block building with no external damage. K-9 walked toward a stairwell that led to the basement. He was about to descend when he noticed that I wasn't following.

"You okay Mutt?" he asked.

I wasn't okay. I felt like I'd been sucker punched in the stomach. Next to the building were three rusted cages next to a pile of trash that included soiled mattresses, dented metal buckets, broken dildos, and splintered dog collars. These were the leftovers from when the Young Wolfz had kept the Buckhead Wives as their sex slaves.

"It's nothing," I said through gritted teeth. "Let's see this place of yours."

We entered the basement. The air was cool and crisp. I could hear the hum of a generator. K-9 flipped on the overhead light. We were in a large room with cinder block walls and a concrete floor. A few boxes sat against the far wall next to a rolling metal door. As we walked toward the metal door, our footsteps echoed off the walls.

K-9 pulled on the metal door and it glided easily along its well-oiled track. Inside was another large room with cinder block walls and a concrete floor, but this one was furnished.

"Welcome to my humble abode," K-9 said proudly.

He must have salvaged every decent item in the Pound. Oriental rugs covered the floor. Paintings of Nubian princesses reclining with white tigers hung on the walls. The smell of patchouli incense had seeped into the cinder blocks. Leather furniture formed a living room in the middle of the room. In a corner was a king-sized bed with a fake leopard skin blanket. A small kitchen area had an industrial sink, a mini-refrigerator, a stove, and a breakfast table.

K-9 walked to the kitchen and lifted a teapot from the stove.

"Ya'll want some hot tea?"

"Sounds good," Venus said, "But first, I'm tired, dirty, cold, and I got to pee like a fucking horse."

"I feel ya."

K-9 took us to another part of the basement where there were restrooms and a place to shower. It made me wonder what sort of business had been in here before the Young Wolfz took over. After we cleaned up, K-9 took us to a small office with stacks of boxes filled with Atlanta Falcons fan wear. The

Georgia Dome wasn't far from here so there was no mystery as to how he'd managed to get his hands on these clothes. The real mystery was why he didn't wear this stuff all the time.

Soon, we had all shed our wet muddy clothes for Falcons red jerseys and black sweatpants. It was a testament to Venus' curvy body that she made these bulky clothes look sexy.

Back in the main room, K-9 filled the teapot with water and turned on a burner. The gas hissed and blossomed into a blue flame. While we waited for the water to boil, Venus and I checked out a long industrial table next to the living room. It was laden with an odd assortment of items and a set of tools. On closer inspection, I saw that K-9 was building bongs and pipes. His completed bongs and pipes filled two sets of shelves. There were bongs made from baby bottles, test tubes, Tupperware containers, saltshakers, liquor bottles, Legos, Tic Tac containers, Nintendo controllers, and a female mannequin head in which you had to put your mouth on her lips and suck in the smoke. There were beautifully crafted pipes of wood, clay, and bamboo.

Venus studied the bongs and pipes, picking up the more unusual ones for closer inspection.

"You made all these?" she asked.

"Yeah," K-9 said. "It's my hobby."

"What do you do with them?"

"Smoke dope. Give 'em to friends."

The teapot whistled and K-9 removed it from the burner.

"You ever think about selling them?"

"I don't know. It's just something I do for fun. What kind of tea ya'll want? I hope you want English Breakfast 'cause that's the only kind I got."

"English Breakfast is my favorite," I said. Actually, I preferred Earl Grey but really who gave a fuck?

"Now if I was your business manager," Venus said, "I could make us some serious money selling this shit."

"Yeah, maybe. Pick one out and we'll smoke a bowl."

K-9 poured hot water into three Falcons coffee mugs and dropped a teabag into each one. Venus studied the collection and picked out a handgun with a metal bowl attacked to where the rear sight had been.

"Good choice," K-9 said.

He carried the three mugs over to a coffee table in front of the couch. Venus sat on the couch and I sat in an easy chair across from her. K-9 sat next to Venus. She handed him the handgun bong and he scooped a round screen from a metal box on the table and fitted it inside the bowl.

"You sure you won't shoot off your face when you light that thing?" Venus said.

"Naw," K-9 said. "I took out all the shit inside. It's just a shell now."

"That's too bad."

K-9 either ignored the burn or missed it. Next to the metal box of screens was a Nike Lebron shoebox. K-9 flipped the lid to reveal that it was full of weed. I wasn't near the box and I could smell the resin. This was obviously his good stash.

I sipped my tea as K-9 loaded the bowl, handed the bong to Venus, and lit it for her. She sucked on the barrel like she was giving it head, held the smoke, and then coughed it out. She blinked a few times and shook her head.

"Damn, that is some killer shit!" she said.

I took the next hit. She wasn't lying. This was some of the best weed I'd smoked in months. It was so good; it cured my headache.

"Fuck, K-9," I said. "If you have this, then why do you sell shitty weed?"

"You don't expect me to sell good dope? That's for me."

"See, that's why you need me to be your business manager," Venus said. "To school you on how to be a good dope dealer. Lesson number one, if you plan to sell dope and stay alive, then don't be selling no stink weed to gun happy assholes like my brothers."

K-9 choked and then coughed heavily. He staggered to the sink and poured himself a glass of water.

"Rom and Remi are your brothers?" he said as he rubbed his eyes.

"That's right," Venus said. "And they stole my money to pay you. That means you ripped me off and I want my money back."

K-9 drained the glass of water.

"So that's what you meant when you said you wanted your money back. Well damn, girl. I didn't mind ripping off Rom and Remi because they stupid, but I didn't mean no harm to you."

He picked up his suit pants from where he'd left them on the floor and fished the bankroll from his pocket and handed the soggy heap to Venus. She peeled off a dripping wet hundred and held it between her forefinger and thumb. Rolling her eyes, she laid the money on the table to dry.

I probably should have left so that K-9 and Venus could be alone, but after the hot tea and excellent weed I was feeling too warm and comfortable to move. The evening had been jammed pack with angry confrontations and narrow escapes. My body was sore and if I walked home now there was a chance I might run into Rom and Remi. Besides, I was still trying to understand why K-9 was head over heels in love with Venus. Sure she was a sexy beast, but the two of them didn't seem "connected on a molecular level that was cosmic and revolutionary" like K-9 claimed.

I slumped down in the easy chair, crossed my arms across my chest, closed my eyes, and listened to them talk. K-9 asked her questions about herself just as I had suggested. Venus didn't need much encouragement. She went into minute detail about her dreams and aspirations to be a business tycoon. I don't know how K-9 managed to stay interested, but he kept asking appropriate follow-up questions. As for myself, she bored me right to sleep.

I dreamed that I was in my werepanther form and I was chasing a wererabbit. She was a really cute wererabbit and I was eager to catch her so I could screw her brains out. But then she turned into the blonde witch who attacked me in the alley. She changed from hopping to flying and I flew after her. She was cute and I was eager to catch her, but now I no longer wanted to screw her brains out. She had a secret and once I got my hands on her, I was going to force her to reveal it to me.

I was inches away from catching her when I was jerked awake by a loud slap.

"GET YOUR NASTY HANDS OFF ME. I DON'T GIVE NO FREEBIES," Venus screamed.

I opened my eyes to see K-9 sitting on the couch and holding his cheek while Venus stood over him with her hands on her hips.

"But Venus, baby," he pleaded. "We got a connection. We share a true love that transcends time and space."

She shook her forefinger at him.

"Oh no! I don't play that game. You claim to be in love until you get some free trim and then you out bragging to your friends that I'm giving it away. I got a reputation to maintain. That's how I handle my business, see?"

K-9 placed his hands over his heart and gave her his best puppy dog eyes.

"Didn't you feel the connection? I know it was real. I refuse to believe you didn't feel it too."

"Connection? What are you talking about connection?"

"When we made sweet, sweet love at Dawgie Daddy's. I know you dancers are supposed to make us feel special, but something real happened when we screwed. You can't deny it."

Venus' forehead knitted and then her face turned dark.

"I have danced for and fucked a lot of werewolves, but only because that's my job. That's how I make my living. But I remember every werewolf I've been with and I have never danced for you and I have certainly never fucked you."

K-9 looked at me as if he'd lost his penis and couldn't imagine where it had gone. I shrugged because I had no idea where it could be.

"That would certainly explain a lot of things," I said. "All night I've had the feeling that you two didn't fit together."

"But she's the one," K-9 said. "She danced for me and then we connected. We connected!"

In one quick and unexpected move, at least by K-9, Venus wedged the heel of her shoe between K-9's legs. He gasped and his eyes grew wide.

"I should squash that worm between your legs into mush," she hissed. "You got the WRONG GIRL. You know what that means?"

"Nope," K-9 squeaked.

"It means despite all your talk about connections and true love, you can't tell one furry butt from another. Every she wolf dancer looks the same to you."

K-9 stared at her shoe. I could feel his heart breaking.

"You're right," he said softly. "I'm sorry I wasted your time."

Venus eased her foot away and sat on the couch. She patted K-9's knee.

"Don't cry. I hate it when werewolves cry."

"I'm not crying." But he was crying just a little.

"You're not the first guy to fall in love with a dancer. It's what we call an occupational hazard."

"Then why did you go on a date with me?"

"Because you asked me. A date is just a date. It's not a declaration of love. Did you think that just because you bought me dinner and drinks that I was going to have sex with you?"

"No. Maybe."

"You're hopeless."

Venus stood up, stretched, and yawned. Her yawn was contagious. K-9 and I yawned. I could feel that it was late morning.

"It's been an interesting evening, but I need to go home now," I said.

"Yeah, I need to get to work. My shift starts in a few hours," Venus said.

"Come on," K-9 said. "I'll drop you both off."

CHAPTER TEN

The bright sun greeted us as we emerged from the basement. The rain clouds were gone and sunlight sparkled off the puddles in the road. There was a moist feeling in the air. Venus took the passenger seat and I got in the back of the Land Rover. K-9 got in last and the engine roared to life on the third turn of the key.

Venus had to get to Dawgie Daddy's before I had to get to the Black Phoenix, so it was decided to go there first. Dawgie Daddy's was in an industrial park in an isolated part of the city so that it would be on neutral ground.

The steady rumble of the car made me drowsy and my eyelids drooped. For once, Venus wasn't talking non-stop about her plans to start a financial empire. She leaned over the front seat and poked me.

"Didn't you get enough sleep last night?" she teased.

"No," I said. "Somebody woke me up when she slapped my friend's face. That was a damn loud slap too. What exactly did K-9 do to deserve such a brutal response?"

"He grabbed my tit," Venus said.

K-9 snickered.

"Was it just one tit or both?"

K-9 and Venus laughed.

"Just one," Venus said. "That was enough. The guys do like my big titties. You know all about my big titties don't you Mutt?"

She poked me again. I glanced at the rearview mirror. K-9 glared back at me.

"What's she talking about?" K-9 said.

I could feel what was about to happen and it sent a chill down my spine.

"Mutt fucked my titties," Venus said plainly.

"When did he do that?"

"After you ran out of the club to avoid getting your ass handed to you by Rom and Remi."

I wanted to cast a spell that would muzzle Venus, but the damage had already been done. The ugly truth was out like a stinking pile of shit.

"Why are you doing this, Venus?" I asked.

"What are you getting so upset about?" she asked. "We've already established that I'm not the she wolf K-9 fell in love with."

"But at the time, I didn't know that."

"When he was fucking you, I believed you was my boo," K-9 growled. "A brother ain't supposed to fuck a brother's bitch under any circumstances. Shit, Mutt. All this time I thought you was my friend, but it was all bullshit."

"I'm sorry, K-9. I don't know why I did it."

"That don't mean shit."

"You're right. I have no excuse."

K-9 slammed on the brakes and the car skidded to a halt. We were in one of the last remaining shadow zones, areas where nothing lived. A ghost town used for shady deals and the perfect place to avenge bruised egos.

"Get out of my car!" K-9 demanded.

I got out. I was looking at a long walk home, but then I deserved it. I expected the car to speed away and leave me in a cloud of dust, but instead K-9 turned off the motor and joined me.

"What are you doing, K-9?"

"We're going to settle this shit right here right now!"

He pulled off his jersey and struggled out of his sweatpants. The Young Wolfz tattoo on his chest had faded into his dark skin.

"I'm not going to fight you," I said.

He kicked off his tennis shoes.

"You got that right. It's just going to be me putting the hurt on you."

Venus climbed out and rolled her eyes.

"Why you got to do this?" she said. "You're making me late for work."

I walked away from the car and headed back toward the city. Naked, he ran past me and blocked my path. His muscles tensed in preparation to transform. Just as the first tufts of fur began to sprout on his chest, the blonde witch landed behind him. Her face was contorted with rage as she raised her hands. There was a crackling in the air. I cast a protective barrier over K-9 and me just as she threw a stinger spell at us. It bounced off the barrier, but because she was so close to us, the energy vibration knocked us off our feet and we skidded across the asphalt road. I got road rash on my forearm, but K-9 lost a swath of skin off his ass.

The witch stormed over to the barrier and pressed her hands against it.

"If you think you can burst my barrier," I said, "you're about to learn differently. The backlash is liable to blow your fingers off."

"You don't scare me," she said. Her fiery rhetoric was ruined by her soft, girly voice.

"Clementine!" Venus shouted. "What in the name of sweet Mother Wolf are you doing?"

The witch ran to Venus and flung her arms around her. They kissed tenderly and Venus stroked the girl's hair.

"When I saw you leave with that guy I got jealous," she said.

"You were stalking me?" Venus asked.

"I know I shouldn't have. You went into the club with one guy and came out with another. That put terrible ideas in my head. I tried to chase him away, but I didn't realize he was a wizard. And then, you took him inside your house. You never take your dates home."

"It wasn't like that. I'd explain but then we'd be out here all damn day."

"I'm sorry I blew up your tree. I lost my temper. Then your brothers ran outside and shot their guns at me. I had to defend myself. I'm sorry Venus, but I hate your brothers."

"That's okay. Everybody hates my brothers."

I got to my feet and offered K-9 my hand. He smacked it aside and stood on his own. I released the barrier. As he went to retrieve his clothes, I saw that his ass was bleeding.

"You don't have to sell yourself anymore," Clementine said. "I'll find a way to take care of you."

"Even if you could, I wouldn't let you," Venus said. "I hate dancing and I hate dicks, but I've been taking care of myself since I was a pup and I will continue to do so."

"You're so brave and determined. That's part of why I love you so much."

Now I understood why Venus pushed so hard to be somebody's business manager. She was desperately trying to create a place for herself in a world that couldn't see past her big tits.

I walked toward them with the intention of introducing myself. Clementine went into defensive mode and pushed Venus behind her. This wasn't easy because physically they were opposites. Venus was voluptuous while Clementine was a stick.

Venus wrapped her arms around Clementine's stomach.

"Don't worry, sweetie," she said. "Mutt's okay for a guy."

"Hello," I said. "I'm Mutt."

"Clementine. Sorry I tried to kill you."

We shook hands.

"That's alright. Happens all the time."

K-9 moped over to us. He'd put his clothes back on. His eyes darted back and forth as he offered Clementine his hand.

"Hey, I'm K-9 Loopy."

"Venus told me about you. She said you were very nice."

K-9 smiled shyly and scurried to his car. He didn't get in. He just stood next to it.

"Okay," Venus said. "Now that everybody has cooled down and we've stopped trying to kill each other, I need to get to work."

"I'll fly you there," Clementine said.

"Girl, you know I get airsick."

Clementine giggled. "That's right. Last time I took you flying, you puked on a man's head."

"I'll carry you," K-9 said. "I was going to anyway."

"Do you mind if Clementine rides along with us?"

"Naw. Get in."

Venus got into the passenger seat and Clementine climbed into the back seat. I stood on the side of the road and waited for them to leave. The engine didn't want to start, but K-9 managed to convince it. He pulled up beside me and rolled down the window.

"Ain't you coming with us?" he asked.

"You told me to get out of your car."

"Now I'm telling you to get in the car. We can settle our shit later."

I got in the back seat next to Clementine. The way I saw it, the crazy shit had come to an end and soon we'd all go back to our normal lives. As usual, I was wrong.

CHAPTER ELEVEN

Venus and Clementine stood outside Dawgie
Daddy's, kissing, hugging, and giggling over private
jokes. K-9 and I sat in the car and watched them.

"They got a real connection," K-9 said. "I
never went looking for that kind of connection. It
found me. But if I can't even tell which bitch I stuck
my dick in, then I don't deserve the kind of love those
two have."

"You're being too hard on yourself," I said.

"I ain't taking advice from you. I should never
have come to you for help. I was a damn fool, but no
more."

Venus and Clementine finally parted.
Clementine flew away and then Venus waved
goodbye to us before entering the building.

"Listen, K-9," I said. "You're right. I have
fucked up every relationship I've ever been in and
you have no reason to listen to me, but hear me out.
The dancer you thought you connected with works
here at Dawgie Daddy's. You have to find her and see

if she feels the same way about you. She might be in there now working this shift. You owe it to yourself to go inside and find out."

K-9 tapped his fingers on the steering wheel.

"Alright. I'll do it," he said. "But you got to come inside with me."

"Really? I can't wait here in the car?"

"I don't trust you to sit out here by yourself. You done already stole enough shit from me."

That stung, especially since I didn't even like Land Rovers.

"I deserved that," I said.

We got out and K-9 glared at me as he locked the doors. As we approached the club, I could hear shouting and assumed the men were cheering on the dancers.

Inside, there was mayhem.

In the center of the main room two female werewolves fought, biting and scratching each other viciously. They knocked over tables and chairs, toppling over bottles that smashed on the floor. Venus was one of the fighters, but I didn't recognize the other she wolf.

The men had formed a circle around them. They held dollar bills in their hand as they bet on who would win. Instead of breaking up the fight, the bouncers joined the betting.

"I got twenty on Venus. Ain't nobody meaner than that bitch."

"I'm putting fifty on Geneva. She gonna tear Venus' head off."

Dawgie Daddy came huffing and puffing out of his office and used his enormous gut as a battering ram to get through the crowd.

"Fighting ain't allowed!" he shouted. "Stop this foolishness!"

But then he saw how much money had been bet on the fight and made an instant rule change.

"The house gets ten percent of the proceeds regardless of the outcome of the fight!"

Venus lifted Geneva off the ground and heaved her across the room. Geneva hit the wall outside the DJ booth, reducing it to kindling. The DJ leaped out of the booth and scrambled to where K-9 and I were standing. I sort of knew the DJ. He went by DJ Two Paws. He was good, but in all modesty he didn't come close to my talent and skill.

"How did this get started?" I asked.

"Man, bitches always be fighting about something," DJ Two Paws said.

"Well, that's open to discussion, but what started this fight."

"The second Venus stepped inside the door, Geneva shouted, 'That bitch stole my man!' And then she transformed and leaped at Venus. Venus barely had time to change before the bitch was on top of her."

We had to swiftly scoot to the side as the she wolves rolled past us leaving tuffs of fur in their wake.

"Look," I said, grabbing K-9's arm and pointing. "Their coats are almost identical. They're both silver and black. It would be easy to get them confused."

K-9 squinted at them and then nodded slowly. He stepped back and transformed, ripping out of his clothes. He jumped over the men and landed in the middle of the fight.

"Stop!" he howled as he pushed his way between them. "There's been a terrible mistake and it's all my fault."

"About damn time you got here and talked some sense into this fool," Venus spat.

Geneva lunged at Venus, but K-9 got his arms around her and pulled her to the ground.

"I fucked up," he said. "You were the one I wanted. You felt the connection, didn't you?"

Geneva struggled to get loose, but K-9 held on tightly. She and K-9 gazed deeply into each other's eyes.

"I can tell from the way your dick's getting hard that you're trying to make a connection right now," she said.

They laughed and rolled around on the floor. Venus transformed back to human. She had bleeding cuts on her breasts and legs. She limped to the dancers' dressing room to attend to her wounds.

The men were furious that there was no clear winner. They argued and shoved each other until Dawgie Daddy stepped in and told them to chill the fuck out or else he would ban them from the club forever. They chilled out and he was very pleased with himself until someone pointed out that since the fight ended without a winner, then all bets were off which meant ten percent of nothing for the house.

"Why the hell do I even bother to leave my damn office," Dawgie Daddy groused as he waddled away.

K-9 and Geneva transformed to human and sat naked at one of the few tables not destroyed in the brawl. She asked him questions about himself.

DJ Two Paws eased into his damaged booth and started playing music as the bouncers picked up the broken chairs and tables and swept away the broken glass. I went to the dancers' dressing room to check on Venus.

Dancers surrounded her, dressing her wounds, and bringing her cocktails from the bar. I recognized Jade, China, Coco, Unique, Unique Two, Jasmine, Tease, and Mizz Booty from back when I was still doing DJ gigs at Dawgie Daddy's. I pulled up a chair and joined them.

"I was going to warn you," Mizz Booty said. "Geneva had been bitching since yesterday that you stole her man."

"That's what I don't get," Venus said. "The girl knows I prefer pussy over dick."

"It's not like she didn't know that you was a player," Jade said.

"Shit, she ain't no different than us," Tease said. "The men use us and we use them. That's the game."

"I still can't believe Geneva actually jumped on Venus," China said. "The girl is always stoned out of her mind."

"She does love the chronic," Tease said.

"Did you see the way the men were betting on who was going to win the fight?" Mizz Booty said.

"Sheeit!" Jade said. "Did you see the gleam in Dawgie Daddy's eyes when he saw the money they were waving around? You know he's going to want us to fight each other."

"I can see it now," Venus said. "Friday nights will be Fight Night with an undercard and a main event."

"Yeah. Dawgie Daddy will make all the money and we'll get all the bruises," Mizz Booty said.

Venus' eyes grew wide. She came over to me and pulled me to my feet and away from the other dancers.

"I got a business proposition for you, Mutt," she said.

"Venus, I already told you that I don't want a business manager."

"That's not what I'm talking about. Now hear me out before you say anything."

I did hear her out. I'm glad I did.

CHAPTER TWELVE

Six months later, I was sitting in my office when the phone rang. The caller ID told me it was Dawgie Daddy. I knew why he was calling. He wanted to bitch about the same thing that he'd been bitching about for the last three weeks. I was sick of listening to him vent, but I valued our friendship too much to ignore the call.

"Hey, Dawgie. What's up?"

"Nothing's up," he boomed. "I'm sitting here with my dick in my hand because I ain't got no damn customers. That bitch is putting me out of business."

"I don't believe that. Is there really nobody there?"

"The place is dead tonight. How long before every night is like this."

"I wouldn't worry. Werewolves will always want werewolf pussy."

"She begged me to make her my business manager. I should've listened to her."

"Yeah, you should have."

"She's ruined me. Won't be long before she does the same to you."

"Calm down, Dawgie. She's not ruining either one of us."

He pissed and moaned for another fifteen minutes before he ran out of steam and hung up. Ed had been napping on the couch across from my desk. He sat up and yawned.

"Was that Dawgie Daddy again?" he asked.

"Yeah."

"Poor bastard. We should go or we're going to be late."

I put on my denim jacket and checked the inside pocket to make sure my flask was in there. We went downstairs to the club. Other than the diehard drinkers at the bar, the place was empty. Pinky was behind the bar reading a paperback novel.

"Pretty damn slow for a Friday night," I said. "Can't blame it on the weather. It's a beautiful night."

Pinky grinned. "It's early."

"Ed and I are going now."

"You better be back in time to play some music. If not, I might have to hire DJ Two Paws to take your place."

I staggered back with my hand over my heart.

"That was mean. Really, really mean."

Ed and I stepped outside and breathed in the cool night air. We stopped at the Mexican restaurant. Only two tables were occupied, but the owner didn't seem worried. I ordered two Café de ollas to go. Then we went into the produce market. I got two apples in a paper sack. At both places, I offered to pay, but was told that my money was no good there.

At the end of the block, on the corner of the Peachtree Street and Marietta Street was the William-Oliver Building, a grand art deco structure. A sign over the main entrance read, "The Venus Flytrap." Below the sign was a poster advertising that evening's events. It was an impressive list.

FRIDAY NIGHT FIGHTS FEATURING:
UNIQUE VS. UNIQUE 2
MIZZ BOOTY VS. TEASE
CHINA VS. ASIA
AND THE MAIN EVENT:
GENEVA VS. SABRINA

People stood in line at the ticket booth. Vampires, werewolves, witches, wizards, and humans waited to buy a ticket. Ed and I walked past the ticket booth to the entrance. Remi stood at the door taking tickets.

"Can I see your ticket?" he growled.

I handed him the apple. He laughed and took a big bite as we walked past him. There was another crowd of people in the lobby. Ed and I sauntered over to the gift shop. Signed photos of the fighters were lined up along the wall. On the opposite wall was a sign that read *Bongs By K-9 Loopy*. I looked over the bongs in the display case. A salesgirl finished selling a signed photo of Tease and came over to us.

"There aren't many bongs in here," I said.

107

"We keep selling out," she explained. "We should have more soon."

Clementine rushed over to greet us. She wore a tuxedo and two-tone wingtips. Her blonde hair was slicked back. She gave me a hug and scratched Ed's neck.

"We were just discussing the shortage of bongs," I said.

"They've been selling so fast K-9 had to hire assistants to help him build them," Clementine said. "I'm trying to get him to set up a shop in Brookhaven. He needs to expand, especially now that Geneva is expecting."

"And she's still fighting?"

"Tonight is her farewell performance. Besides, they don't really fight. Everyone must know its fake."

"Doesn't make it any less fun to watch."

"K-9 is going to be a father," Ed said. "Never thought I'd be saying those words."

"I know right?" Clementine said.

We went into the main arena. I had worked with the construction crew to turn this place into a fighting venue with stadium seating. A traditional wrestling ring would never hold two werewolves, so this one was the size of a basketball court.

Clementine led us to the first row. It was roped off for reserved seating. She pulled the rope aside for us to enter. I caught a few werewolves staring at us. Most likely they were trying to figure out if we were someone important or better yet if we had access to the fighters after the show.

"I have to get ready," Clementine said. "I'll see you guys later."

She hurried off. I opened the lids to the two Café de ollas, took out my flask, and added Tequila to them. I put one of the cups on the floor. Ed took a test sip and flicked his tail. I tasted mine. He was right. It needed more Tequila so I emptied the flask into both cups.

Ed and I chatted about nothing while the stadium filled up. The crowd roared when the house lights were lowered. Spotlights lit up the ring.

Clementine and Rom entered and stood in the middle. He was dressed as the referee with a stripped shirt and black slacks. Clementine carried a microphone.

"Are you ready for Friday Night Fights at The Venus Flytrap?" she said, her amplified voice bouncing off the walls.

The crowd cheered and stomped their feet.

"Our first match tonight is between two mighty she wolves with two things in common: the same name and a burning hatred for each other. Unique and Unique Two!"

They strutted in from opposite sides of the arena. They were in their werewolf form. Their fur had been brushed to a glimmering sheen. They waved at the crowd and snarled at each other. Clementine stood between them. She was a petite woman already, but they made her look like a doll.

"The loser tonight has to change her name!" Clementine announced, which brought the crowd to their feet. She peered up at the werewolves. "Now I want a clean fight. That means you can bite, scratch, spit, and mutilate, but no name calling and no stealing each other's boyfriend!"

Clementine hurried out of the ring. Rom stood between the werewolves until the bell rang, and then he hurried out of the way. Unique grabbed Unique Two and tossed her across the ring. She crashed to the floor, but was quickly back on her feet. They rushed at each other and the scratching, biting, and spitting began in earnest. There was no mutilation. There never was. In fact, the first two weeks they had the fights, there was a problem with the fighters getting the giggles in the middle of a bout. And in one memorable fight, the werewolves started wrestling and ended up making love.

Since then, Venus had managed to get the fighters to remain in character throughout the bouts. Even though anyone could tell the contests were faked people still bet on the matches. Venus was fine with that as long as the house got ten percent of the take.

I didn't see Venus and didn't expect to see her. She was behind the scenes, making sure everything ran smoothly.

The Venus Flytrap's weekly fights were a big benefit to my block. After the show tonight, most of the crowd would eat at the Mexican restaurant, shop at the produce market, or come to the Black Phoenix. Our businesses were connected to each other.

Unique lost the match and announced that she would change her name to Destiny. The fighter known as Destiny came running out and challenged Unique's right to use that name. They almost fought it out right then and there, but Clementine stopped them and said that there would be a match next week to decide whose destiny it was to be called Destiny.

Ed and I stayed for Mizz Booty versus Tease, but left before China took on Asia. The arena had gotten hot and sweaty with so many excited people jammed together so the night air felt deliciously cool.

"This is one of the few times one of your adventures has had a happy ending," Ed said.

"That's true," I said. "K-9 made his connection with Geneva and Venus made her connection with... Who did she connect with?"

"Herself. She had wanted to be somebody's business manager, but what she really needed was to be her own boss."

"Everybody found their true love but me."

"Oh for fuck's sake, Mutt. It doesn't always have to be about you."

The End